THE WEALTHY ONES

BY
LOREEN CLOPTON-MASON

To order additional copies of this book, contact:
Xlibris
844-714-8691
www.Xlibris.com
Orders@Xlibris.com

ISBN: Softcover   978-1-4500-2852-3
         EBook   978-1-4771-7498-2

Print information available on the last page

Rev. date: 03/14/2023

Snap, Stitch and Von are three mice who had been living at the Human's residence for a very long time when one day Snap became determined to see how other humans - mainly the "wealthy" ones - lived.

Snap had overheard Mr. And Mrs. Human talking
about wealthy people, bosses, mansions and many other
things that he and his brother and sister were
not familiar with.

"That boss human must have lots and lots of goodies throughout the place. It would be grand if we could go and explore the premises and see what we can find to eat." Snap said.

Von looked at Snap with a disgraceful shrug, and

asked, "Don't you think that you are being a bit

greedy? We have more than enough to eat already.

There IS always food around here for us...

in almost every corner!"

Snap turned to Stitch, who has never agreed with him before, and asked; "Wouldn't you love to see how those wealthy humans live?"

"...This is not just about getting more food, but it could be a learning experience," Snap continued... "Besides, we have not gone anywhere since we moved in." "Yes, you are right!" Stitch explained.

"What?!" Von yelled. "You are actually agreeing
with him? Are you serious?"

"Calm down," said Stitch; "We should venture out to see what's going on. Maybe we could learn something from this. Let's consider it a field trip."

Early the next morning, the three of them hid inside
Miss Human's very large bag that she always carried
with her when she went to Boss Human's house.

Von and Stitch both frowned when Snap started to
nibble at something that was wrapped in foil.
"Stop that! You have eaten already," they snapped in
a sharp whisper. "OK, ok! Sorry about that.
It's a habit."

After what seemed like hours, the mice noticed that they were no longer in motion; and it was silent.

Stitch said, "I guess we are here. Let's wait for a
minute or two and make sure that the coast is
clear before we get out."

Finally, Stitch signaled to Snap that he could check to
see if everything was ok , Snap quickly climbed to
the top of the bag, peeked around, jumped out,
checked every nearby doorway and corner,
then yelled; "Come on out guys! You're not
going to believe your eyes!"

Stitch and Von wanted to scream with excitement, but
contained themselves so not to make too much noise.
Once they were completely out of the bag, they
joined Snap; and the three of them just stood
there in total disbelief.

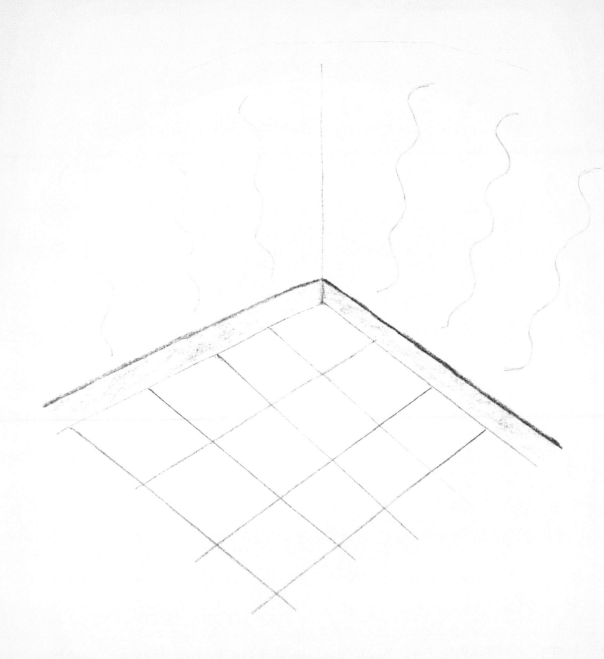

The place was huge and very bright, but there was
not a single morsel of food or goodie anywhere
to be seen.

They decided to look around the huge house; each
going in a different direction. Moments later, they met
up together, but neither had found anything that
amounted to much.

Snap was appalled; he asked... "What is this? Wealthy
humans must not eat or something. Where is the food?
All the goodies? Is this for real?

Stitch decided that they should just get back
into the bag and go home.

Later that night Snap, Stitch and Von were
discussing the events of the day. "You know what?"
Snap asked. "Compared to that house we were in today;
I feel that *we really are the wealthy ones.*"

Printed in the United States
by Baker & Taylor Publisher Services